This fiction book is dedicated to all of the world's racers, to the men and women who risk their lives in the name of motor sport. The grit and determination they show is outstanding and honourable, it would be a very different world without them both past and present, and this story focuses on the past and no doubt bears some resemblances to many lives in the racing world; so a big thank you to all of you, you are all champions in one way or another.

Author Derek Crysell

Art work by Derek Crysell

Credit to Baz & Jo Budden for the pictures of Baz actually racing his Norton at the Isle of Man.

With thanks to my family Ali, Harry & Laura for putting up with me whilst I toiled away at the writing desk, love you all forever, D.

Jo Buddens Dad, Baz Budden riding his Norton at the Isle of Man TT, how inspiring he is.

Tom, Grandad and Elle walked hand in hand back towards Toms Dads van , Elle stopped to pick up her bright blue scarf that she had tied around Grandads arm earlier. Tom asked his Grandad "How are you feeling"? Grandad said, "Quite sore to honest Tommy boy, I took a hard knock there, but I suppose I'll be ok".

Elle was crying, "What's up with you old girl? Don't worry about the Norton, we can fix that up again" said Grandad. "You silly man" cried out Elle, " we could have lost you, you could have died, you're sixty five years old Rod, sometimes it feels like you think more of that bike than you do of me". "No, no Elle, I could never love anything as much as I love you, you were my first love and always will be". Elle and Grandad stood on the tarmac close together and cuddled each other, Elle holding her bright blue scarf and Grandad still in his buckled suit of armour.

A police van, ambulance and fire engine turned up at the same time, the ambulance crew wanted to check Grandad over first but there was a problem, his suit of armour had been buckled so badly they couldn't undo it, the Fire Chief came over and said "there's only one thing for it, we will have to cut it off" "Cut it off" Said Grandad, "yes cut it off" said the Fire Chief. "Right" said the Chief to his men, "get him on his back carefully" Grandad was protesting "Do you know how much this cost me? It's an original suit of armour this is, from the days of King Arthur himself I'll have you know". The Fire Chief smiled and then started to laugh; Grandad said "What on earth could be so funny at a time like this"? The Fire Chief tried to hide his laughter and then composed himself just long enough to say "So why has your original suit of armour have made in China stamped on the soles?" And then he burst out laughing again.

The suit of armour was duly removed and there was Grandad left wearing only his string vest and his bunny rabbit print boxer shorts and stripy socks, the ambulance crew checked him over and said they want to take him back to hospital for a scan. His racer pals helped pick up all the pieces of the Norton 500 and put it all in the back of Toms Dads van, Elle went to hospital with Grandad, the burglar was taken away in the police van, and Sargent Thoroughgood travelled back in the van with Tom and his dad.

Back at Grandads house they unloaded the broken Norton 500 into the barn workshop. What a sorry mess it was in, the front wheel had collapsed, the forks were bent beyond repair, handle bars bent, the framework was twisted really badly and the engine casing was cracked, the side car was a write off.

Tom stared at the heap of broken parts, Toms Dad stood next to him. Tom said "Dad, do you think grandad can mend all of this? I mean it's all a bit of a mess really isn't it"? Toms Dad shook his head sadly and said "I nearly lost my dad today; I never want him to ride again". And with that said; the barn doors were closed together and the darkness swept over the broken Norton 500 as it lay on its side in a pool of its own oil, that evening the moon looked through the barn window and shone for a while on the faithful number four.

8pm Toms house phone rings, "Dad; its Nanny, she's still at hospital with Grandad, she wants to talk with you". Elle talks to Toms Dad quietly on the phone so Tom can't hear her and says "It's not good news I'm afraid they scanned him and done some tests on him and he has a really weak heart, they said we are lucky to still have him after the crash today, he is staying in overnight and I am staying too, we will get a taxi home in the morning, good night love".

"Dad, what did Nanny have to say"? Asked Tom. "Oh she said they are keeping him in overnight to make sure he's ok, now get to bed Tom it's been a really stressful day".

Tom went to bed thinking about Nanny and Grandad having to stay at the hospital overnight, his tummy felt all horrible and whirly, Tom prayed Grandad would be alright and then gently fell to sleep.

The next morning Tom went to do his paper round, he arrived at the paper shop and was astonished to see a picture of his Grandad in his suit of Armour on the front page of the Norfolk Bugle newspaper. The headline read: **Bungling Burglar Blighted by Big Bold Brave Knight in Shining Armour.**

The interview was given by the petrol station lady (the nosey woman as Grandad would say)

Tom raced round to deliver the papers and get home again so he could find out about his Grandad. Tom got home and saw his Dad washing his car in the driveway, "Hi Dad, have you heard any news about Grandad? He's on the front of the newspaper." Toms Dad looked at the copy that Tom had brought home and said "Goodness me how cool is that Tom?" "Yes we had a call from Nanny and they coming home this morning by Taxi, I did say I would pick them up but Grandad said he didn't want all that fuss.

At 11am Toms house phone rang, it was Nanny saying they were now leaving and will be home in an hour. Tom, his Dad and Mum went to Grandads house to meet them when they got home. Grandad didn't look very well he seemed pale and not quite himself, they helped to get him indoors and sat him on his sofa, whilst Toms Mum helped Elle to prepare some lunch. Tom came through to the living room with the newspaper to show Grandad the front page.

The whole family sat down to lunch just being glad to be together. After lunch Tom, Grandad and Toms Dad took a walk down to the barn where the Norton was. Tommy opened the bar doors and Grandads heart sank when he saw his beloved Norton 500 laying on its side all bent and buckled and broken.

They started sorting out the mess by putting the parts into piles, the sadness in Grandads eyes said everything to Tom and his Dad, that Norton 500 had been with him for 50 years, there really wasn't much to mend, there wasn't much that wasn't damaged.

Grandad sat on his stool by his workbench and bowed his head slowly shaking it from side to side. Toms Dad said, "Come on Dad, let's leave this for tonight and have a good think in the morning.

As they all went indoors again Elle was about to turn the television set off when the evening news came on; and the announcer said "and a wonderful story from yesterday has just been delivered to us on film by hand, lets run the tape and see what we have". It was actual film footage of the burglar chase and how the TT Racers drove down the burglar and it showed the speed that the Norton was doing when it crashed into the red Ferrari and what happened to Grandad.

The film was taken by the lady from the petrol station on her camcorder from the sidecar of one of the motorbikes. The announcer said "This man is a hero and this film has shown the whole of Britain how fearless he was in stopping the thief, we believe he is Rod Coleman the winner of the Isle of Man TT race in 1954. Well done Rod we are very proud of you; and now onto the next story".

Elle turned the television off; they all went to sleep for the night. The next morning the phone rang, Elle picked it up and spoke softly "Hello who's calling please"? The person on the other end of the call asked to speak to Rod Coleman, Elle called Rod to the phone, "Hello" Said Rod, "Who is calling please"? "My name is Kevin Whittaker and I am the press officer for Norton Motorcycles, we all saw your story on T.V and we were just calling to see how you are and how your Norton is". Rod paused for a moment and then said "Well, I'm ok but my Norton is practically beyond repair, and because it was not road legal I am not covered on insurance, so it looks like it will never be ridden again".

Mr Whittaker continued, "we would very much like to come and see you and your Norton as it is such a historic bike, and we feel we owe that to you at least; Would be possible for us to come and see you in a couple of days"? Rod said that would very nice to meet you"; "Then that's settled", said Mr Whittaker, "We will see you in a couple of days".

Grandad could not face going into his workshop so he sat indoors not really wanting to do anything; he kept thinking about his actions and how different things could have turned out, if only he hadn't have chased after the burglar he would have still had his Norton in one piece.

On Wednesday morning after breakfast, Elle heard a low rumbling noise coming down the road, she thought it's not bin day today and looked out of her kitchen window, then she excitedly said "Rod, Rod, come and see what's backing into our driveway". Rod came through to the kitchen window and saw a huge black lorry backing in and as it turned to get straight Rod saw on the side written in big gold letters, "The Norton Racing Team" all of a sudden Elle and Rod had goose bumps all over them because of the excitement. The lorry stopped and the big hiss from the airbrakes suggested it was staying put. The cab door opened and a team of six men got out all neatly dressed in their Norton Racing Team uniforms. Just then an electric blue colour Jaguar XJS pulled in the driveway in front of the lorry, a rather tall slim man got out of the jaguar, and he was wearing a blue suit white shirt and red tie and very shiny shoes.

He walked up to the front door and knocked gently. Elle opened the door and the man introduced himself, "Hello my name is Kevin Whittaker, we spoke on the phone two days ago", Rod came to the door and they shook hands, Rod said so where are you off to with that big lorry then"?

Mr Whittaker said "Well if it's alright with you; my team want to stay here and rebuild your Norton 500 for you, free of charge, we have every spare part you could ever wish for in the back of that lorry, when we saw the news report and saw what you did; we all agreed we have to help this Hero out, and help that Norton go on for another fifty years. The idea came from our managing director". "So where can we find your Norton Mr Coleman"?

Rod lead the way to the workshop, he seemed to have found a spring in his step again, his eyes seemed brighter too Elle thought to herself. The team followed Rod Down to the workshop and opened the big barn doors and there they stared at it, just looking at this iconic Champions pride and joy lying on its side. "Well this won't do, this won't do at all, oh dearie me", Said Mr Whittaker, "Right lads, get to work and lets save this piece of beautiful machinery.

Grandad stepped back with a huge sense of relief and watched the Norton Team strip his bike down and get to work on it. Elle was up and down the driveway several times during the three days the team were there with flasks of tea and homemade cakes and sandwiches, she really enjoyed seeing these guys help Grandad out in getting his beloved Norton 500 back together again. The frame of the bike was so badly twisted that they had to start from scratch with a new frame, new wheels and tyres, new forks and handlebars, brakes, Headlight and speedo, the petrol tank was still ok though. Grandad asked the guys not to mend the sidecar as he won't need it anymore. At the end of the three days the famous number four was back together again, the Norton team had even made a new fairing and painted a big number 4 on it just as it used to be. Grandad couldn't thank them all enough, his pride and joy sat there in front of him once again, leaning on its stand just gleaming. Before Mr Whittaker left he handed Grandad and envelope and told him to keep it safe for when he needed it, he shook Grandads hand and winked as he left.

 Everyone was so pleased for Grandad; he had his beautiful Norton 500 back. That night after tea, Toms dad spoke to Grandad, he basically told Grandad that he didn't want him to ride the Norton anymore due his heart condition. Grandad asked them not to tell Tom as he didn't want him to worry about it all.

A couple of weeks went by and Grandad had been nipping down to his workshop to start the Norton , you know , so it didn't seize up , he said it wasn't to hear the exhaust pipe going WOM, WOM, WOM, at all.

One night when Grandad was in his workshop alone he opened the envelope that Mr Whittaker had given him, Grandad slowly pulled the letter from the envelope, and on the headed note paper it read "Free pass to race at the Isle of Man TT Races", goose bumps went all over Grandad and his hands were shaking at the thought of having another crack of the whip, his mind took him back to the early days of blasting around that track with the wind hitting his face, the feel of his leathers, the shifting of gears with his bikers boots on, in his mind he was back on that track, laying almost flat on the petrol tank to get a few more miles an hour of that thundering Norton 500. Suddenly Tom's dad opened the barn doors and startled Grandad, "what have you got there in your hand"? He asked, Grandad said "Oh just a copy of all the parts they used to rebuild the Norton", Well you better come in now dad you'll be catching a cold.

A couple more weeks had passed and Grandad asked Elle to telephone Tom and ask him to drop by as he wanted to see him, Tom dropped in to see Grandad the next day after his paper round.

Grandad was in his workshop when Tom arrived, "Hi Grandad" "Hi ya Tommy boy how are ya"? "I'm ok thank you; Nanny called and said you wanted to see me". "That's right I do want to see you Tommy, now I've got something to ask you, now I know you have been good to me and I think the world of you, but you have to keep this secret to yourself, do you understand? If you can't keep a secret then I can't ask you".

"Grandad, I can keep a secret, what do you want to ask me"? "Well you know the Norton team came and fixed my bike up don't you"? "Yes I do".

"Well here it is then, Mr Whittaker gave me an envelope when he left, and I opened it yesterday and inside it was a free pass to race at the Isle of Man TT whenever I wanted to". Toms jaw dropped wide open. "But Grandad its dangerous , you're not as young as you used to be , I mean its quick there and it's not even a proper track , they are just country roads, there will be loads of young riders there, how will you cope with it"?

"Tommy boy I'm not going to race, you are". "I can't go Grandad I'm too young". "How old are you now Tommy? You must nearly be sixteen soon". "I'm sixteen next month". "Good that gives us two years to prepare you for it". "How are we going to do that Grandad"? "Well I've been having a good old think about this, now what we will do is this". Grandad started to explain to Tom that over the next two years he will pick Tom up on the Norton and go for a little ride each week and that they would stop off at a disused air field and that's where they would do the training; doing things like changing gear, bike control, starting and stopping, how to speed safely, and how to lean at speed, and how to lay on the tank to become more aerodynamic. At the end of the conversation Toms eyes were so wide open Grandad thought his eyes were going to pop out. "Now there's one more thing Tommy boy that I've got to tell you".

Tom's heart sank; he thought to himself; when people say things like that its normally bad news. "Tommy, I want you to have the Norton, I'm getting too old to ride it but I can give you all the knowledge you'll need to have a good chance in the race". "I don't want to take your Norton away from you Grandad it's been with you forever; it's your life","Well Tommy boy you can live the rest of it for me in that case; you're the only one I trust to look after it". Tom hugged Grandad long and hard and a tear ran down Grandads cheek.

The next Saturday morning and true to his word; Grandad turned up at Tom's house on the Norton with a spare helmet, Toms Dad came out and asked "Where do you think you two are going"? Grandad quickly said "We are just spending some time together every Saturday from now on, we are just going for a nice steady ride around the coast road; you can't deny me that surely"? Tom didn't say a word, he just popped the helmet on and got on the back of the Norton; put his arms around Grandad and off they went nice and slowly. Tom's Dad waited in the driveway to hear the distant roar of the engine, but there was nothing apart from the faint noise of the engine getting quieter as it got further and further away.

They arrived at the disused airfield, it was a sunny morning and nice and dry, Grandad stopped the Norton and Tom got off, Grandad put the stand down and leant the Norton over slowly to the left until the stand touched the ground, he switched the engine off. Tom Said "right can I have a go then"? Grandad looked at him and smiled; "Let me ask you some questions first Tommy boy; what safety checks do you need to do first"?

Tom looked at the Norton with squinting eyes and his tongue was poking out of the side of his mouth whilst he took a moment to think; then he blurted out "Check the tyres are pumped up, make sure I have enough fuel, check the oil is ok see if the lights are working"? Not bad Tommy boy, not bad at all and they both laughed. Grandad showed Tom where to check the oil and how, he showed him all the things he needed to check before riding a motor bike; Tom took it all in, he was a bright lad.

Grandad said "you get on the back again, and you watch my left hand and left foot, when we get going, and you can see that I have to pull the left handle before I change gear with my left foot, and let the left handle out again slowly; so just watch that bit first while we go up and down the runway.

Week after week Tom and Grandad went for their secret ride out to the airfield, then on the fifth Saturday Grandad said, "Today is the day you get to have a ride on the Norton my boy", Tommy was thrilled and scared at the same time, Grandad went through all the checks with Tom before he took control of the bike, Tom got on and only just managed to get the Norton off its stand, he didn't realise how heavy the bike actually was, Grandad sat on the back. "Right Tommy boy take me through the start-up procedure". Tom said "Stand is up and away, gears in neutral, fuel pump primed, ignition lights on, front brake on, press starter button". "Marvellous" Said Grandad,

"Here we go then Tommy, press that starter button". Bog, bog, bog, Vroooom snarl, growl, went the engine, "Right let it tick over on its own said Grandad". Tom could feel the throb of the engine though his entire body as it ticked over. "Right first gear selected" shouted Tom. "Ok let's go" said Grandad. Tom pulled the clutch in, hit first gear, wound the revs up and let go of the clutch, the result of that was amazing, Tom managed to pull a wheelie with Grandad on the back and they shot off down the runway on the back wheel of the Norton with the engine revving like crazy; Grandad was swearing and Tom was screaming; eventually Grandad managed to get his foot on the brake and gradually bring them back down to earth. "Pull the clutch in and get it into neutral Tommy then turn it off. "Well I must say that was exciting Tommy boy, where did you learn to do that"? "Don't tease Grandad that was horrendous. I thought I was going to crash it. Grandad couldn't stop laughing then Tom looked at his Grandad laughing his head off and that started Tom Laughing too. Over the next year they spend many hours together every Saturday practising and testing, they got to the level that Tom could get a fast start without pulling a wheelie by shifting his weight forwards over the handle bars to stop the front wheel leaving the ground.

Tom was good at cornering at speed and in fact had become quite confident in handling the Norton 500. Eventually two years had passed and Tom was ready to go to the Isle of Man TT as he had become 18 years old on his Birthday.

One Thursday morning Grandad rang his son, (Toms Dad) and asked if he could borrow the van, Toms Dad said "what do you to borrow it for"? "Oh, I just want to take some bits down to the scrap yard; like my old sidecar, I think it's time I let it go, it's been long enough now". Toms Dad agreed. Tom overheard the telephone conversation and asked "what did Grandad want"?

Toms Dad said" Grandads coming round on Friday to borrow the van, he wants to get rid of his side car and he would like you to help him.

The next day Grandad Walked round to Tom's house to collect the van and Tom, Tom came out of the house and waved at Grandad, Grandad waved and smiled back. "Come on then Tommy boy, let's go and do some stuff", said Grandad.

Tom got in the van and they set off to Grandads house. Tom said "So you getting rid of the old sidecar today then"? "Not exactly Tom, you and I are off to the Isle of Man for the TT Race tomorrow". Tom exclaimed in a rather surprised voice "What? But I thought you were getting rid of the sidecar today"? Grandad looked at Tom and said "This is the last chance we will; or shall I say I will, ever get to see the Norton 500 in full race mode,

so we're going back to mine to pick it up whilst Nanny is out shopping and we are going on the run to the Isle of Man with the Norton in the back of the van". Tom said "But I don't have any spare clothes or riding leathers". "You can borrow my riding leathers Tommy boy, they will be a little baggy on you but will still protect you if the worst happens". As they approached Grandads house, Grandad slammed the brakes on and pulled over. "What's wrong" said Tom. "It's Elle she's just riding her pushbike to the shops, we'll have to wait here for a bit until she's gone".

Tom said "But she'll know you're missing by dinner time and Dads going to go mad when he finds out". "That's the chance we'll have to take Tommy boy".

As soon as Elle had disappeared out of sight they backed the van down the driveway to the workshop; they then loaded up the Norton and strapped it down, they collected the riding leathers and helmet, gloves and goggles, they closed the barn doors and left for the Isle of Man.

Elle got back from the shops and realised Grandad wasn't back home, she rang Toms Dad, "Hello " Said Toms Dad, "Hi its Elle, is Tom and Grandad back home yet?, They have been gone along time I hope they are alright". Toms Dad said "No they are not home yet, they were only going to take the old sidecar to the scrap yard; we will pop over in our car, see you in a moment".

Toms Dad and his mum got in their car and went to Grandads house; Toms Dad went straight down to the workshop and looked through the cobwebbed window. He came running back to the house the house shouting "The Norton's gone" Elle sat down wondering what on earth could be going on, she checked in the wardrobe to see if any of his clothes were missing and then she spotted his cardboard box containing his riding leathers was missing, then she found the envelope from Mr Whittaker stating that Grandad had a free pass to race at the TT Races. "When is the TT Race on?" Asked Elle, Toms Dad said "It's this weekend why?" Elle showed him the letter.

"Oh my goodness you know where they have gone don't you?" Said Toms Dad, "They've gone to the Isle of Man with the Norton, quick call sergeant Thoroughgood" said Toms dad. Tom's Mum Rang the police station and asked to speak to Sergeant Thoroughgood, "Hello Sergeant Thoroughgood Speaking" "Hi Its Tom's Mum, we think Tom and his Grandad have gone to the Isle of Man in our van with the Norton in the back".

 "Well what's wrong with that?" Sergeant Thoroughgood asked. "Well we are really worried, Tom's Grandad has a weak heart and he shouldn't be racing a motorbike at his age, we need your help". Sergeant Thoroughgood said "alight keep your hat on, I'll borrow the police van and we can all chase after them in that, when did they leave?"   "They left about eight o'clock this morning" Said Toms Mum. "Well they have a good five hours head start on us; I'll be round to the house as soon as I can.

   Half an hour later Sergeant Thoroughgood turned up in the police van and Elle and Tom's Mum and Dad got in and off they went heading for the Isle of Man.

   It was such a long along journey they all agreed that they would stop off at Hotel and carry on in the morning; meanwhile Grandad and Tom were taking it in turns to drive the van whilst the other one slept and they arrived at the Isle of Man in good time.

Saturday Morning had arrived, Grandad and Tom had slept in the van with the Norton 500, They had breakfast and used the shower facilities on the site, It would soon be time to get the Norton out; they drove the van to the pits where they had their own little garage and unloaded the Norton, but Tom looked around and saw that all the other bikes were much more modern and the leathers the other guys were wearing were very flashy and smart looking. Tom put on Grandads leathers and Grandad was right, they were baggy, in fact you could have fitted another half of a Tom inside them.

Tom and Grandad were checking the Norton over before the race would start, it was full of fuel, oil was good, tyres great condition; then all of a sudden a couple of other riders came walking past and started laughing at them, Tom got quite cross and said "what's your problem?" Then one of them said "that bike belongs in a museum mate and who's that with you, Your Grandad or something?" Tom went to get up and square up to the guy but Grandad caught his arm and said "Don't worry about their sort Tom, they are not worth it".

As the men were walking away one of turned round and said "That heap will never beat my Suzuki", then he walked away laughing saying to his mate "Did you see what he was wearing, he'll be lucky his suit doesn't slow him down like a parachute on a skydiver, he looks like he's the kid from the sixties, ha, ha, ha".

The announcement came over the tannoy, "Can all riders prepare themselves to be on the grid in ten minutes". The message echoed due to the delay from speaker to speaker.

Tom was nervous, Grandad sensed it and said "Tommy boy take it easy, you're not here to win this ok, don't put yourself in danger, just do what we have practised over the last two years, just listen to my voice in your head, remember to slow down a bit into the bends lean with the bike, accelerate out of the bend, shift your weight over the tank and let it rip down the straight".

"Now let's get you on the grid"

The Race Steward started speaking over the Tannoy "Riders, please ride safely, ride within your capabilities, there is no speed limit, but take care, The winner will be the first rider to cross the line with the quickest speed recorded on the tenth lap, good luck gentlemen.

Sergeant Thoroughgood drove the police van onto the race site and asked the man at the gate where the pits are, the man said "you're too late to join the race it's now going to start".

Tom's Mum, Dad, Elle and Sergeant Thoroughgood walked towards the stands, they met Mr Whittaker by accident on the way and Mr Whittaker said "you can all sit in my special viewing box and I will telephone the pits to let them know you have arrived". "Arrived" shouted Toms Dad "we are not arriving we've come to stop them".

Mr Whittaker said "It's too late you can't go into the pits, just go to my private viewing box and wait there, I'll see what I can do".

Just then the message came over the tannoy for the last time "Riders please start your engines". The noise was deafening, all the high pitch noises coming from the newer machines, Tom hit the electric starter button, bog, bog, bog, bog, bog, bog went the Norton's engine, the horrible Suzuki guy was near Tom and could hear the Norton having trouble starting, he was laughing at Tom again, his face soon turned from grinning to a scared look when the Norton 500 kicked into life with the biggest roar ever,

WOM, WOM, SNORT.

Quite a few of the riders looked round to see what on earth could have made such a noise, and there they saw it, in all its glory; the famous number 4 from 1954

The riders were set off one at a time with thirty seconds between them, the horrible guy on the SUZUKI was two bikes in front of Tom, the two in front then were allowed to start and whizzed away sounding like two wasps in a tin can.

It was Toms turn next, his family and sergeant Thoroughgood had just sat down in time to see the Famous number 4 leave the start like a rocket, the sound was tremendously loud, and the sound from the exhaust sent vibrations through the chest of every spectator standing within range, they all held their chests as the Norton blasted away.

"There goes my Dad" shouted Toms Dad getting really excited and being carried away with the whole experience.

Elle Said "That's not your Dad, that's Tom, them leathers are too baggy for that to be your Dad". Toms Dad looked at his wife and said "Did you know anything about this?" "No I didn't she protested".

Tom took it easy just as Grandad had said on the first Lap then he started to feel more comfortable with the route he had taken, the second lap was quicker the third even faster, Toms Dad sat quietly on the first three laps watching his son go flying past, On the fourth time past the spectator stand Tom could have sworn he saw his Dad jumping up and down in the Executives box and Nanny waving a bright blue scarf.

The laps were flying past, on the seventh Lap the horrible guy on the Suzuki had to pull in for a tyre change and Tom just raced on and gained half a lap on him, but soon the Suzuki was out of the pits and was chasing after Tom.

On the eighth lap Tom Came into the pits, "what's up Tommy boy?" Said Grandad, "it keeps losing power then keeps picking up again" "it's the spark plug lead it's split, let me grab a new one", said Grandad. The new lead was fitted but the Norton wouldn't start, the electric starter had packed in, Grandad said "jump on Tommy boy I'll give you a bump start", Grandad pushed as hard as he could and the Norton fired into life and pulled away like a dog after a cat,

Grandad lost his balance and fell over quite hard as Tommy sped away, he was helped up by another teams mechanics and taken to the executives box in the grandstand to sit with his wife and Family.

On the ninth lap the Suzuki overtook Tom but the horrible guy tried to punch tom in the arm as he went by, Tom got really cross and opened up the Norton's full power, Tom was lying flat on the tank he was at the most aerodynamic position possible and he was gaining on the Suzuki second by second, on to the tenth lap, Tommy was right behind the guy on the Suzuki and noticed the Suzuki's back tyre had a bulge in the side of it and it was making the bike wobble at such high speed then all of a sudden the back tyre blew out sending dust and bits of rubber everywhere, luckily the parts of the tyre missed Tom. The Norton was flat out, the rev counter had gone through the red band, and Tom wanted to win for his Grandad and to prove that the famous number 4 was still the best.

Tom was coming down the home straight the Norton was smoking really badly , the throttle was wide open , the crowd was cheering him on as he came down the straight towards the checked flag , the crowd was going wild and waving flags and shouting his name , the Norton's exhaust snapped open and it sounded like the roar of a dinosaur as he passed the finish line in first position, what a thrilling ride , Tom had won the TT Race on his Grandads trusty Norton 500 , not just any old Norton but the famous Number four.

At the podium Tom received his winning cup; Grandad, Elle, Toms Dad and Mum were beside themselves with joy, even Sargent Thoroughgood was jumping up and down with happiness. Tom came to find his family in the stands, Grandads face was a picture of sheer joy and happiness, Tom gave Grandad the biggest hug ever, everyone who could get near Tom was patting him on the back, they were all shouting "well done Tommy Boy", Tom gave the winning cup to his Grandad and said "hold this for a while Grandad I need the loo".

When Tom came back there was a clearing around where his family were sitting, as he got closer he could see Sargent Thoroughgood leaning over Grandad. Toms Dad tried to stop Tom from seeing but he pushed his way through, Nanny was kneeling by the side of Grandad, holding his hand, she was crying, Grandads heart had given up , he passed away holding Tommy boys winning cup and in view of his beloved Norton 500 the famous number four. A split second later the Norton 500 burst into flames in the pits and was totally destroyed.

A week later Grandad was buried in the village graveyard and just after the vicar had said his final words Elle threw a red rose for him, and just as she did, she could hear the roar of a distant motorbike, and she thought to herself, he's not really gone, he's out there somewhere riding his Norton 500 by the seat of his pants. Tom asked if they could lower his TT Winning cup onto Grandads coffin, Elle held Toms hand, and whispered, "There's no need to do that Tom". Tom said "He deserves it Nanny, he was the real champion". In the back ground were Grandads TT racer pals heads bowed in respect.

And so Grandad went to heaven with Elle's red rose and Tom's TT winners' cup. The Norton Team was at the funeral to pay their respects to one of the world's greatest champions, Mr Whittaker gave Elle his deepest sympathy and handed Tom an envelope and told him to open it when he was ready.

A calm breeze blew across the Norfolk country side and some say in the dead of the night you can hear Grandad on his Norton 500 giving it some teddy.

A couple of weeks passed and Tom sat in his bedroom thinking about Grandad, then suddenly remembered the envelope Mr Whittaker had given him, Tom opened it carefully with tears running down his cheeks, he slid his finger across the envelope and pulled out the letter, it read, "To the winner of the Isle of Mar TT Race, you have not only proved yourself as a professional rider but you are now the proud owner of one of our latest Norton Motorcycles, please give us a call when you are ready to receive your new Norton with our compliments. Signed, Mr Whittaker.

Meanwhile Elle was looking out of her kitchen window staring at the workshop doors just wishing her husband would just come walking out of them and give her that cheeky grin and shout "Pip, pip old Gal" tears came to her eyes and rolled down her cheeks and dripped onto the back of her hand as she leant against the sink. Elle decided to take a walk down the workshop for the first in a while to smell that familiar smell of oil and grease, she opened the barn doors only to find the old sidecar had been made into a flower bed, and it was painted in pretty blue and yellow colours, and it had a sign painted on the side" For My Darling Elle" it even had a number 4 painted on the end, Elle found a seed packet nearby and knew that her Husband had made it for her and planted her favourite flowers in it so she could see them grow each year that passed without him. Then she found a letter addressed to her in Grandads hand writing, it started off with "Pip, Pip Old Gal," Elle sat on the stool near the workbench and read her letter in private.

Two weeks after; Tom was out on his new motorbike, he had just come round a bend onto a straight piece of road and decided to open her up a bit, Tom kicked it down a gear and the forks extended upwards with the power, Tom checked his mirrors and saw that another bike had come round the corner he had just been on, the bike had a big fairing on the front, one headlight on, it was gaining on him really quickly; as it got closer Tom could see the rider was wearing sixties riding gear, including the old style helmet and goggles, a bit closer still and it sent shivers down Toms spine, Tom saw and big number four painted on the fairing; Tom blinked and the bike had disappeared as if it was never there; Tom slowed down , then he noticed there were two shadows on the road, one was his and the other was in the shape of his Grandad, Tom felt a huge sense of calm wash over him, he knew his Grandad was with him, riding side by side for evermore, Grandad was Toms guardian angel keeping him safe on the roads forever.

And the Norfolk breeze blew gently across the fields.

Courage and determination

TT Racing   *is part of*
British history and is being kept alive by
the new racers of our time.

Printed in Great Britain
by Amazon